NODDY'S MYSTERY CAR

This edition first published in Great Britain by HarperCollins Publishers Ltd in 1999

1 3 5 7 9 10 8 6 4 2

For further information on Enid Blyton please contact www.blyton.com

ISBN: 0 00 1361643

Cover design and illustrations by County Studio
A CIP catalogue for this title is available from the British Library.

The HarperCollins website address is:
www.**fire**and**water**.com

Printed and bound in Great Britain

NODDY'S MYSTERY CAR

Collins
An Imprint of HarperCollins*Publishers*

TOY
TOWN
DARK
WOOD

"Oh, I do love my car!" Noddy said to himself as he drove happily through the countryside. "It's the best car in the whole world!" **PARP! PARP!** said his little car in agreement.

"I hope you last for ever and ever," he said. "I'd be so sad if I ever had to swap you for a new car."

Suddenly, Noddy had to twist the steering wheel hard to the right. He pressed the brake right down to the floor –

SCR - E - E - E - ECH!

Noddy was lucky not to smash into a tree. He'd only just stopped in time.

"Sorry, Noddy!" It was the goblins driving a little orange car. "We didn't mean to push you off the road."

"I should jolly well think so!" Noddy shouted at them angrily. "You nearly made me have a very bad accident!"

The goblins stepped out of their car and started to dust Noddy down. But Noddy was still very cross and he just pushed them away.

"You goblins shouldn't be allowed to drive cars!" Noddy snapped at them. "And I can quite see why if you're going to swerve all over the road like that!"

The goblins really did look very sorry. They looked at each other – and then down at their shoes.

"It's not our fault, Noddy!" Sly mumbled. "It's this old car we bought from Sammy Sailor."

"Yes, look at all the rust," said Gobbo. "And everything keeps falling off. It's useless!"

Sly and Gobbo both started to inspect Noddy's car. Now that had no rust on it at all – everything shone and glimmered just like new.

"If we had a car like yours, Noddy, we'd be able to drive really safely," Gobbo told him. "Why don't we just swap?"

Noddy was so shocked at this suggestion that for a moment he couldn't speak. "What? Swap my lovely car for that horrible piece of junk?" he exclaimed. "MOST CERTAINLY NOT." Noddy was cross all the way home.

In fact, he was still cross when he had his sandwiches for tea ... when he had his soup for supper ... when he put his pyjamas on and went to bed.

He was still a little bit cross the next morning!

"As if I would want to swap you!" he remarked to his car as he drove it out of his garage. "I never want any car but you!"

Noddy started to drive along the road, looking for anyone who might want to go to the station or the harbour.

But his car hardly seemed to move. And it kept making loud clonking noises.

CLONK! CLONK! CLONK!

"Aren't you feeling very well today, little car?" Noddy asked it.

Normally the car would answer Noddy with a **PARP! PARP! PARP!** But today it said nothing at all. Not even a very quiet **PARP! PARP! PARP!**

It just kept clonking and clanking.

Noddy was starting to get very worried about his little car.

Especially when the goblins overtook him in their orange car. How could his poor little car be even slower than that old wreck?

"Your car's obviously had its day, Noddy!" Gobbo shouted at him, chuckling. "Take it to the rubbish dump!"

"I just need to take it to Mr Sparks," he told himself, trying to be brave. "I bet Mr Sparks will make it good as new again!"

But Mr Sparks could only shake his head and tut when Noddy's car finally chugged up to his garage.

"I'm afraid there's nothing I can do for your little car, Noddy," Mr Sparks told him as he peered under the bonnet.

"Everything's far too rusty," he added as he wheeled himself underneath the car on a little trolley.

Noddy could not hold back the tears any longer. He was about to bend down and hug his car, when Mr Sparks accidentally scratched the paintwork with his spanner.

"That's odd!" he remarked. "This car is painted orange underneath!"

Noddy thought it very odd, too – but then he suddenly realised what had happened.

"Come on, little car!" he said. "We're going to find the goblins!"

The car went so slowly that it took Noddy a long time to find the goblins. But at last he spotted them. They were parked near the Zebra crossing.

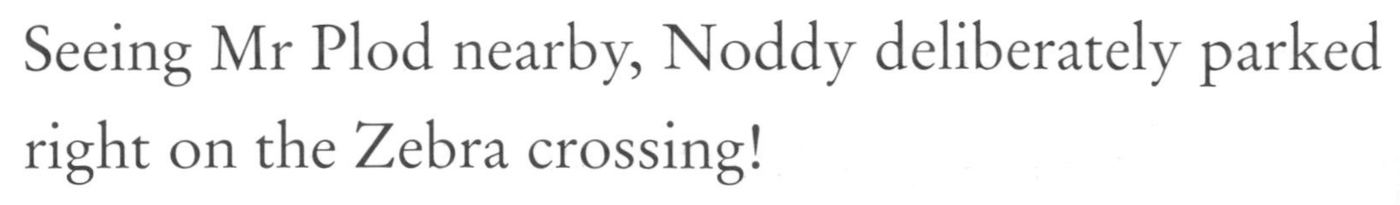

Seeing Mr Plod nearby, Noddy deliberately parked right on the Zebra crossing!

"You can't park your car there!" Mr Plod shouted, running up to him. "It's against the law!"

"But it isn't my car," Noddy remarked. "*That's* my car!"

He was pointing to the car the goblins were sitting in. He marched straight up to it and carefully scratched off some of the paint with the edge of a sixpence.

Mr Plod gasped as a streak of yellow appeared.

"What's going on here?" he asked, taking out his notebook.

"The goblins swapped my car with theirs while I was asleep last night," Noddy explained. "They painted my car orange so it looked like theirs – and their car yellow so that it looked like mine!"

Mr Plod immediately arrested the goblins, leading them off to prison. He told them that secretly swapping cars was a very serious offence!

Meanwhile, Noddy drove his car straight to Mr Sparks's garage so that it could be painted yellow again.

"It won't take long," Noddy told the car, "and then we'll have a day off together. We'll go for a nice drive in the country. Just you and me."

PARP! PARP! said his dear little car happily.